THE HOUSE
THAT JACK BUILT

For John

First published in the United States by
Ideals Publishing Corporation
Nashville, Tennessee 37214

First published in Great Britian by
William Heinemann Ltd.
London, England

Printed in Hong Kong

Library of Congress Cataloging-in-Publication Data

Falconer, Elizabeth.
    The house that Jack built.

    Summary: A rebus version of the cumulative nursery
rhyme about the chain of events that started when
Jack built a house.
    1. Nursery rhymes. 2. Children's poetry. [1. Nursery
rhymes. 2. Rebuses.]. I. Title.
PZ8.3.F2Ha   1990   398.8   90-4467
    ISBN 0-8249-8459-5   CIP
                                                  AC

THE HOUSE
THAT JACK BUILT

A rebus book designed by

E L I Z A B E T H   F A L C O N E R

IDEALS CHILDREN'S BOOKS
Nashville, Tennessee

This is the

That Jack built.

This is the malt

That lay in the

That Jack built.

This is the rat

This is the cat

That chased the rat

That ate the

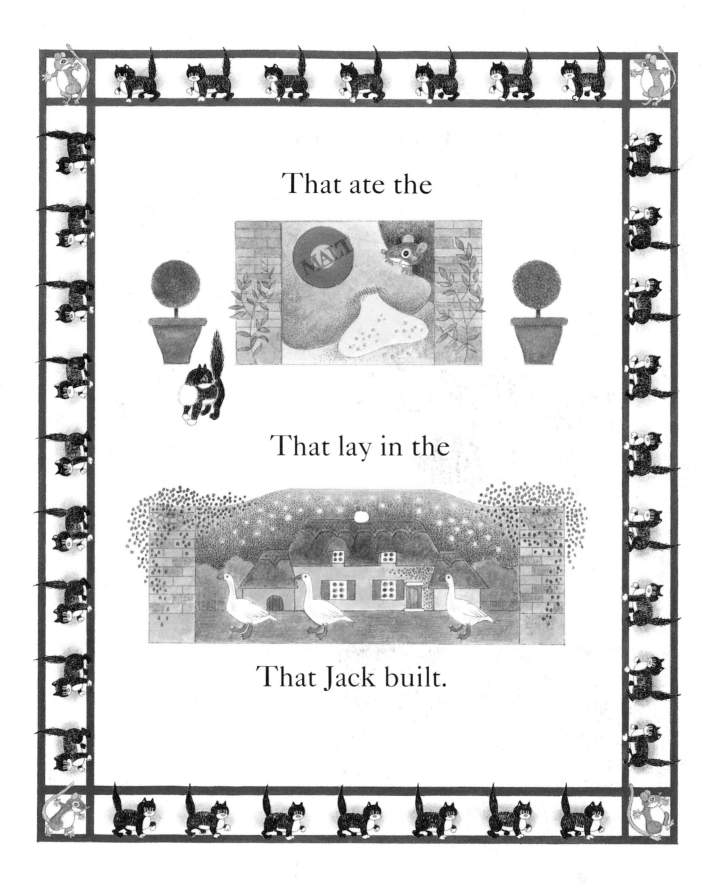

That lay in the

That Jack built.

This is the dog

That worried the cat

That
chased
the

That ate the

That lay in the

That Jack built.

This is the cow with
the crumpled horn

That tossed the dog

That worried the   That chased the

That ate the

That lay in the

That Jack built.

This is the maiden
all forlorn

That milked the cow
with the crumpled horn

That tossed the

That
worried
the

That
chased
the

That
ate
the

That lay in the

That Jack built.

This is the man all
tattered and torn

That kissed the maiden
all forlorn

That milked the

That tossed the

That worried the

That chased the

That ate the

That lay in the

That Jack built.

This is the farmer
sowing his corn

That kept the cock that
crowed in the morn